羅茲的房間

Rosie's Room

Mandy and Ness

Chinese translation by David Tsai

在羅茲的房間裡有許
多值得看的東西。
透過她的放大鏡
羅茲可以**研究** . . .

There are lots of things to
look at in Rosie's room.
Through her magnifying glass
Rosie can **study** . . .

透過窗戶

用她的望遠鏡

羅茲**瞭望**到 . . .

Looking through the window
with her binoculars,
Rosie **spies** . . .

當太陽發出光芒的時候
羅茲用 . . . 遮擋著
她的眼睛。

When the sun shines

Rosie **shades** her eyes

with her . . .

羅茲目不轉睛地**盯著**水
中的東西。那是 . . .

Rosie **stares** at something

in the water. It's . . .

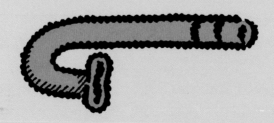

透過照相機羅茲**看著**
前方。她拍攝了 . . .

Rosie **looks** through her
camera. She takes . . .

羅茲**凝視**著被子裡
的什麼東西？

What is Rosie **peeping**

at under the duvet?

"瞧！" 羅茲說道。
"你**看到**了誰？"

"Look!" says Rosie.
"Who do you **see**?"

"你看到
了我!"
"You can
see ME!"

For Mart.
N.

Rosie's Room / English–Chinese

Milet Publishing Limited
PO Box 9916, London W14 0GS, England
Email: orders@milet.com
Web site: www.milet.com

First English–Chinese dual language edition published by
Milet Publishing Limited in 2000
First English edition published in 1998 by Scholastic Ltd

ISBN 1 84059 159 5

Typeset by Typesetters Ltd, Hertford, England
Printed and bound in China